My mum said that while
everybody was sleeping
the wall was made,

and when we woke up, Dad was stuck on the other side.

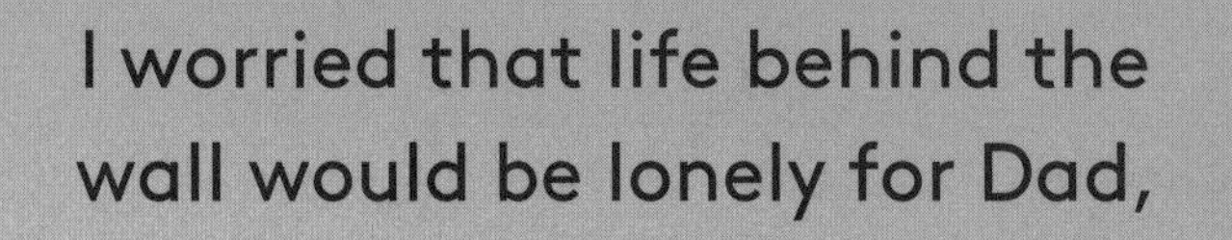

I worried that life behind the
wall would be lonely for Dad,

but Mum said that things
were better over there.

And we couldn't leave, anyway.

Every night, I dreamed of
Dad breaking through the
wall and rescuing us.

But every day
I woke up and the wall
was still there.

I spent every minute dreaming of ways to get to the other side.

I wasn't the only one. All around me people were trying to cross the wall...

in all kinds of inventive ways.

Some people were lucky.
Others were not.

But I knew I had to do something,
or we might never see Dad again.

CENSORED

So, I found a
hidden spot near
the wall, and I
started to dig.

Day by day my tunnel
got deeper and deeper.

RIGGS

Finally, when my tunnel was ready,
we made our escape.

We were frightened, but wouldn't
give up until we reached Dad.

All we had to do was get to the tunnel undetected. We were nearly there...

when we were
frozen in our tracks
by a thunderous
voice calling,

"HALT!"

I trembled with fear as
I spoke to the soldier,

but I shouldn't
have judged him
so quickly.

He said nothing should come between a father and his family,
and he let us go.

We pushed through the crowds

to a small house on a quiet street.